For the two who make my flock complete. I love you Lucas and Poppy!

In a faraway land of Seashell Isle,
lived Flamingo Fran with a fabulous smile.

Fran was happy as can be,
enjoying the sun and the big palm trees.

'Til one day Fran noticed a little frog,
crying alone on the edge of a log.

Fran asked the frog,
"Why are you so sad?
Whatever did happen?
It must have been bad!"

The frog looked at Fran with a tear in his eye,
and then let out a sad little sigh.

"I have no friends and don't know what to do.
No one will play with me. I feel so blue."

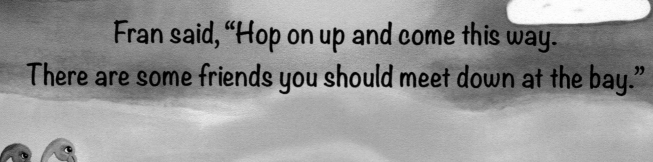

Fran said, "Hop on up and come this way.
There are some friends you should meet down at the bay."

Fran took the little frog to meet her whole flock. "Can I have your attention?" She said with a squawk.

"This little frog is need of some friends."
The flock looked at Fran and said, "Well, that depends..."

"Can that frog have fun, scream, and shout?"
And with one LOUD RIBBBBBBBIT, he let it come out!

"I'm a nice little frog who loves to have fun!
I love to run and jump and soak in the sun!"

Fran was so happy and full of glee
as she saw them all playing under the palm tree.

Fran felt so proud of her very good deed...
It's great to be kind and help those in need!

Every day since on Seashell Isle,
Fran and the frog play and smile.

Because they had learned and truly believed that a flock of good friends is all you need!

Made in the USA
Monee, IL
11 February 2021